Animal Surprise!

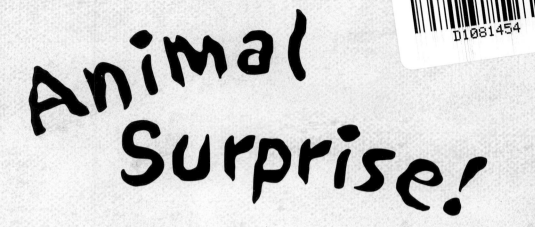

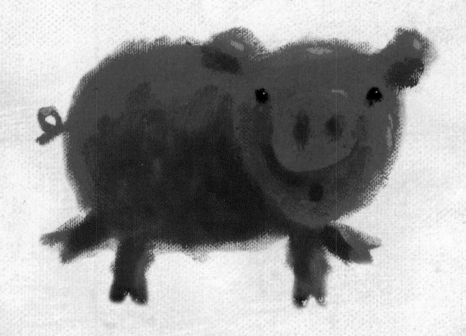

Christopher Gunson

Picture Corgi

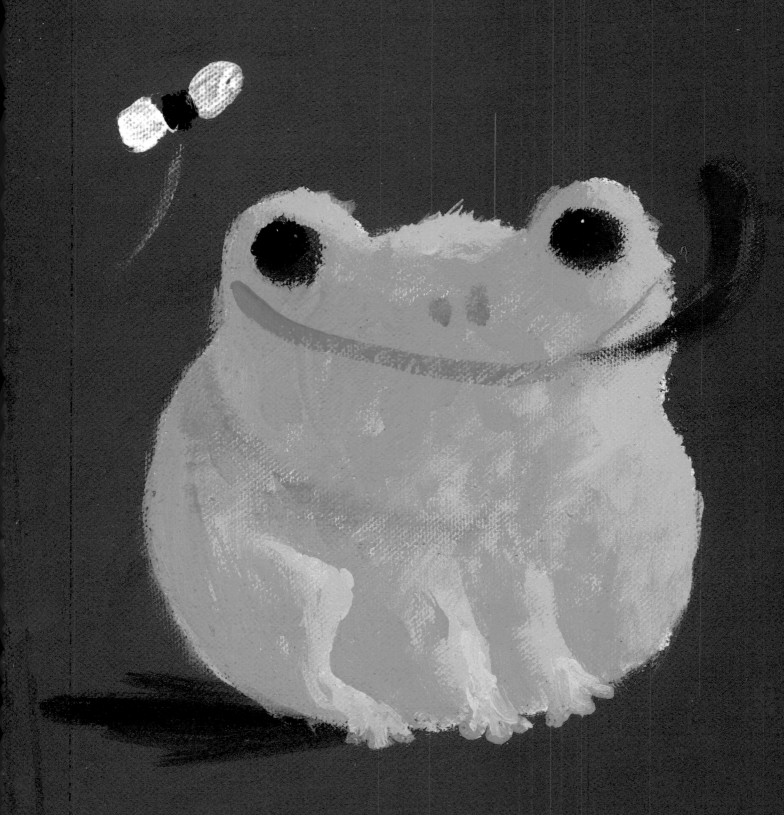

Flick

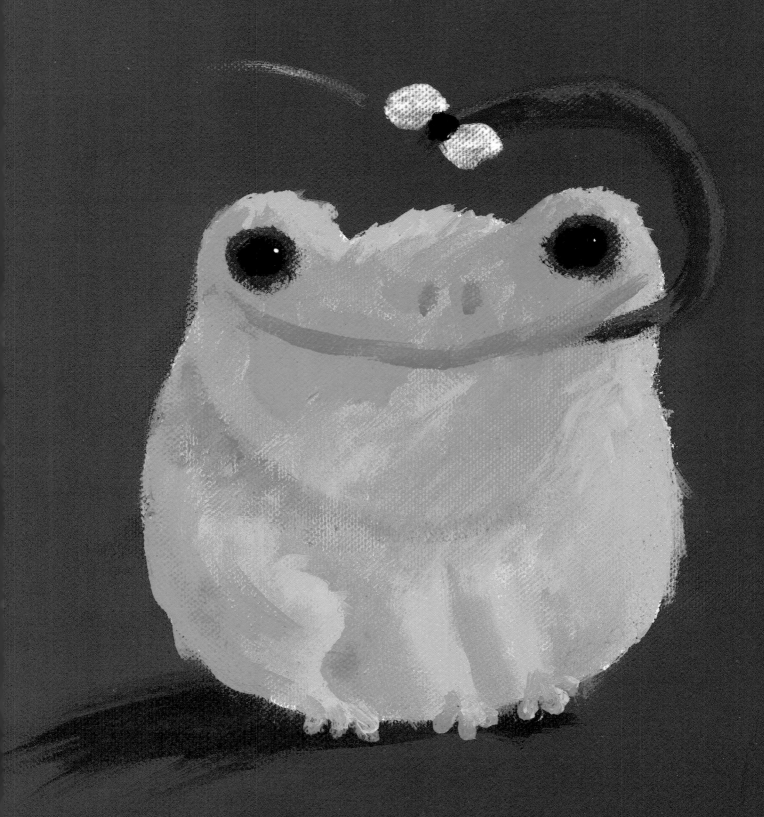

Stick...

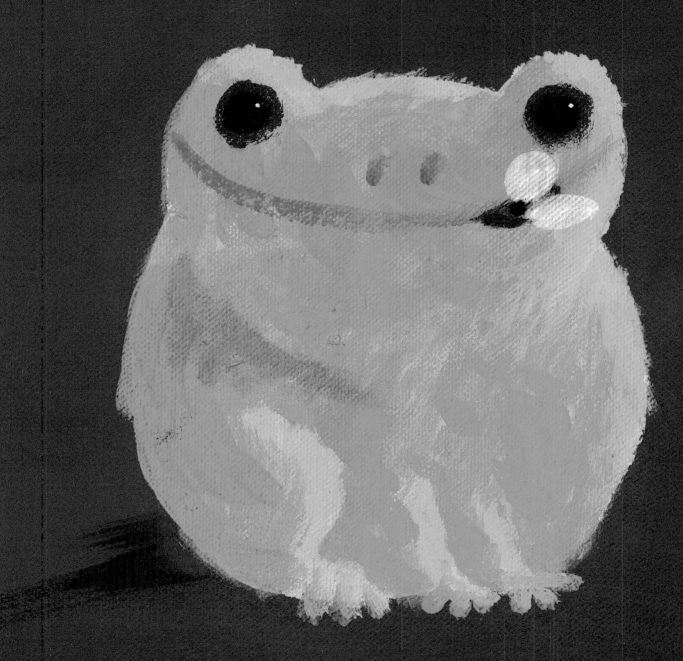

Yum!

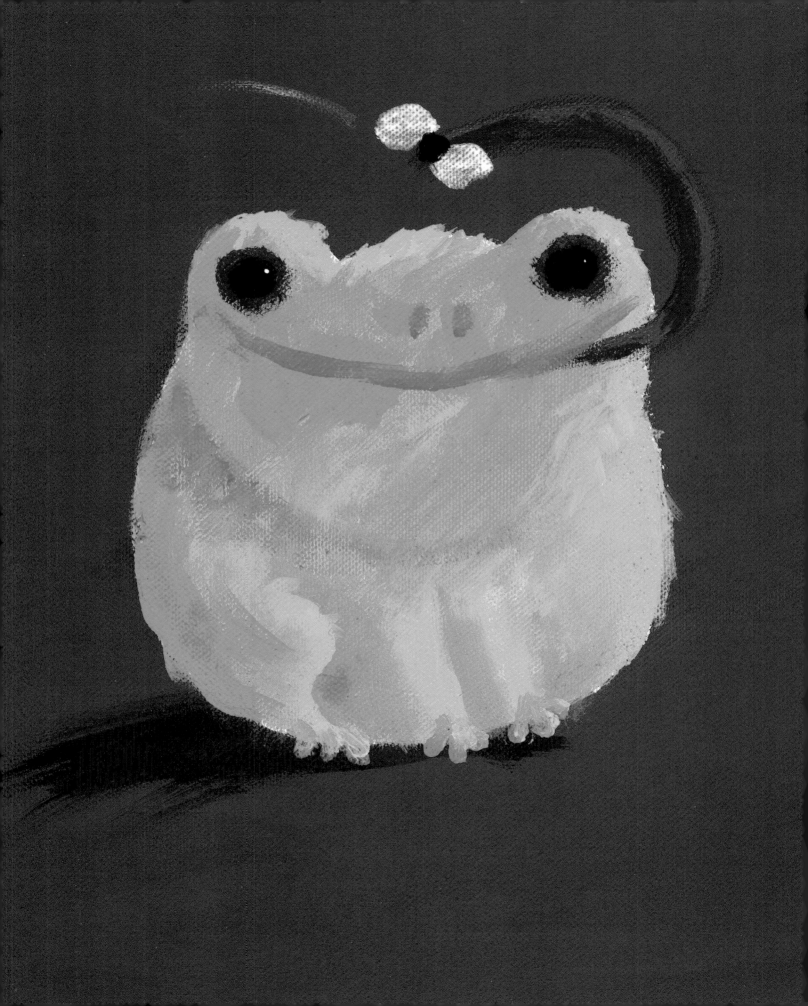

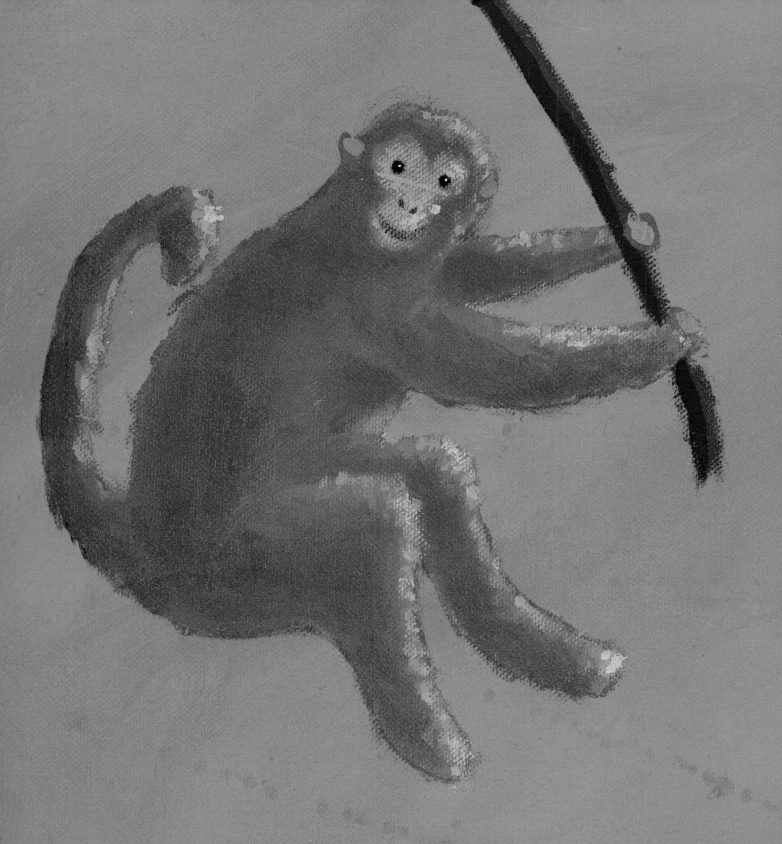

Swing

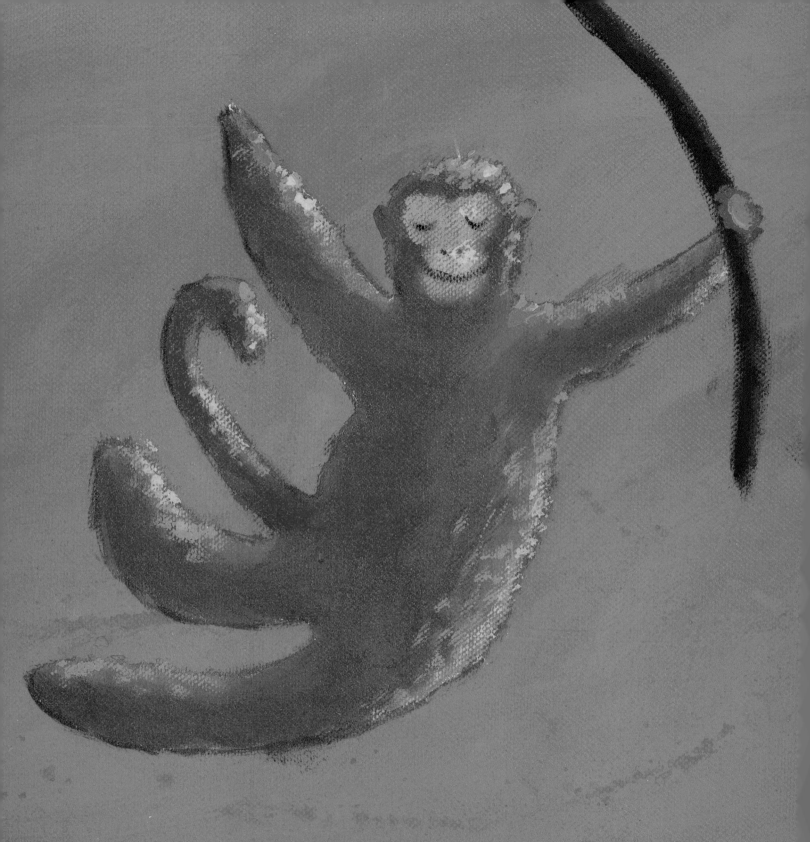

Swoop...

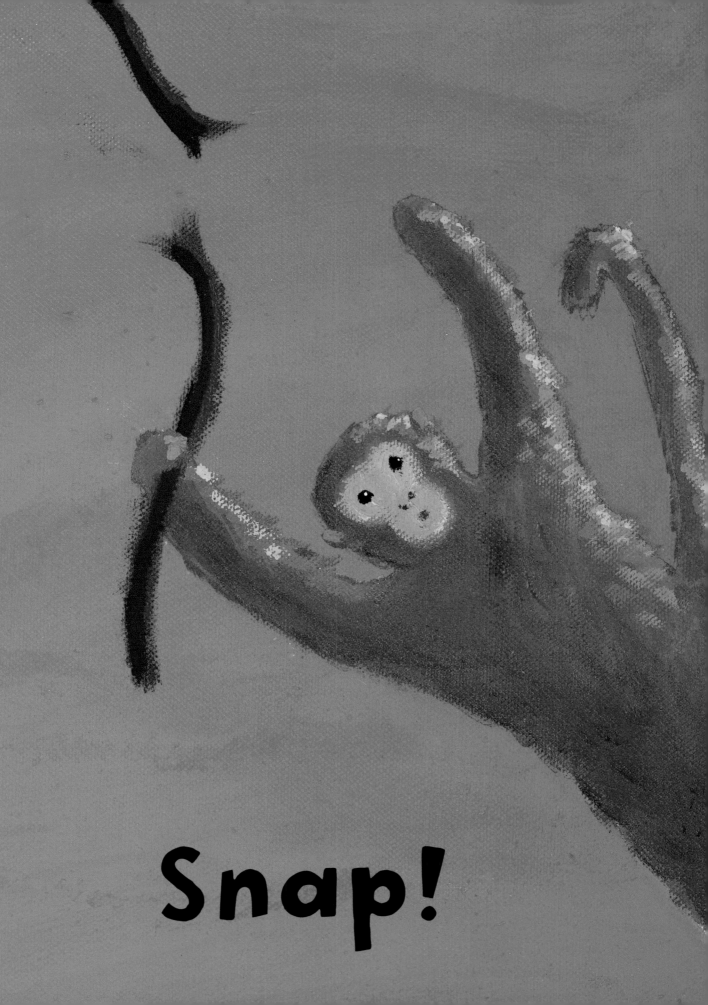

Snap!

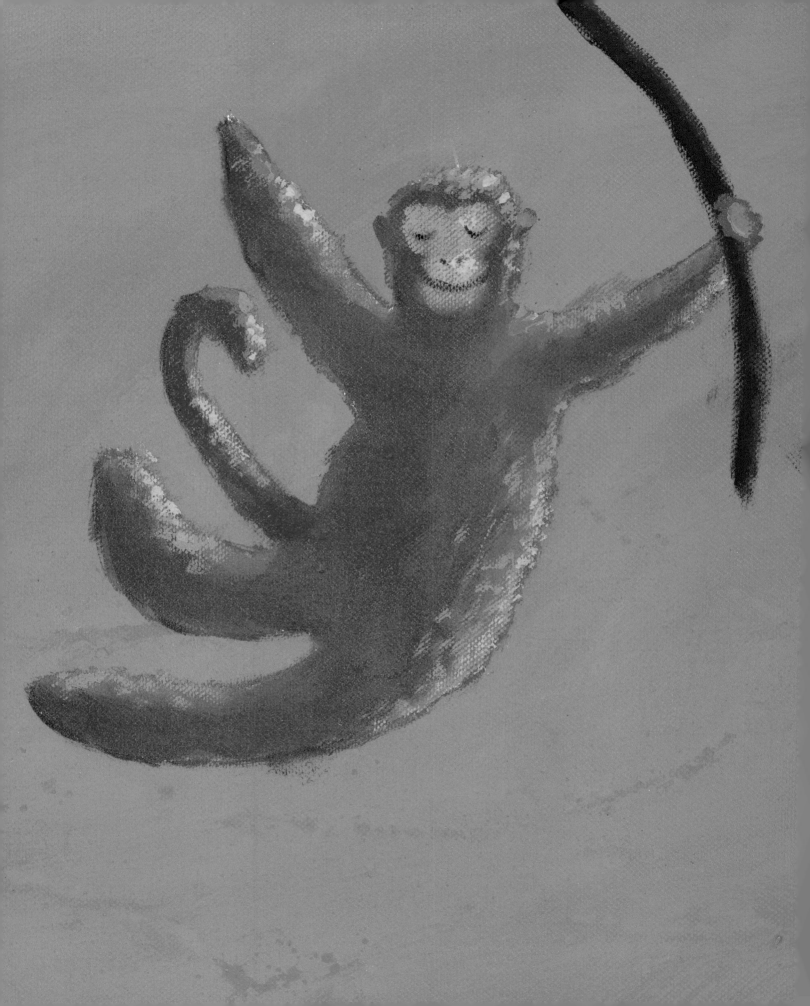

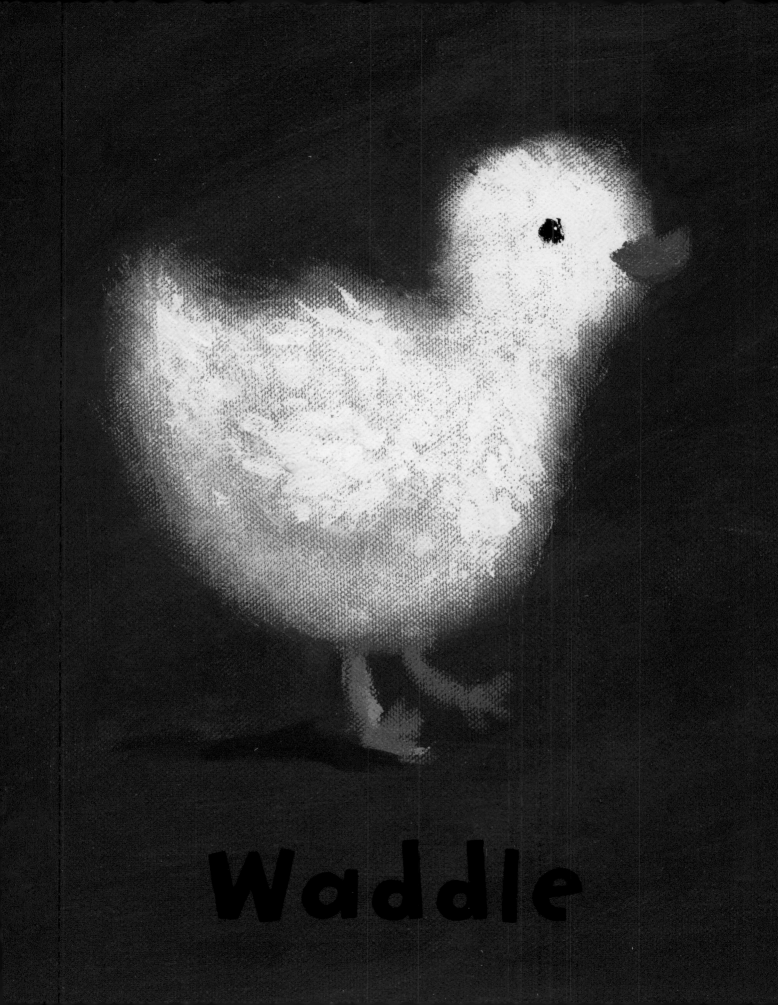

Waddle

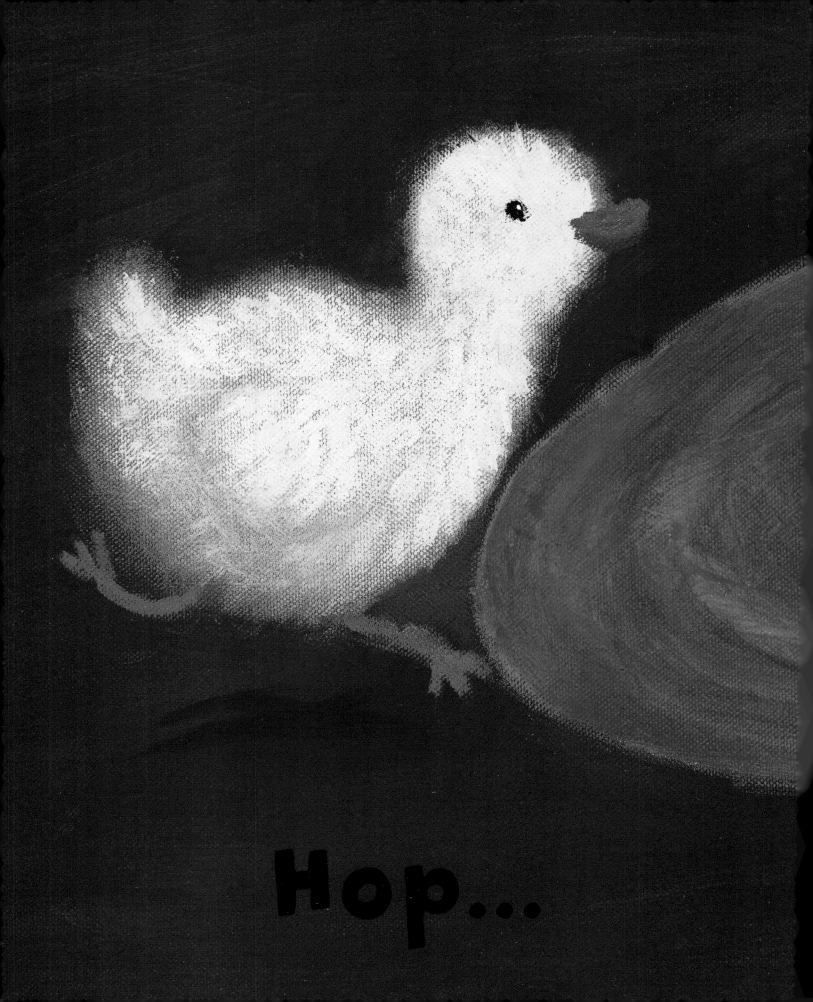

Hop...

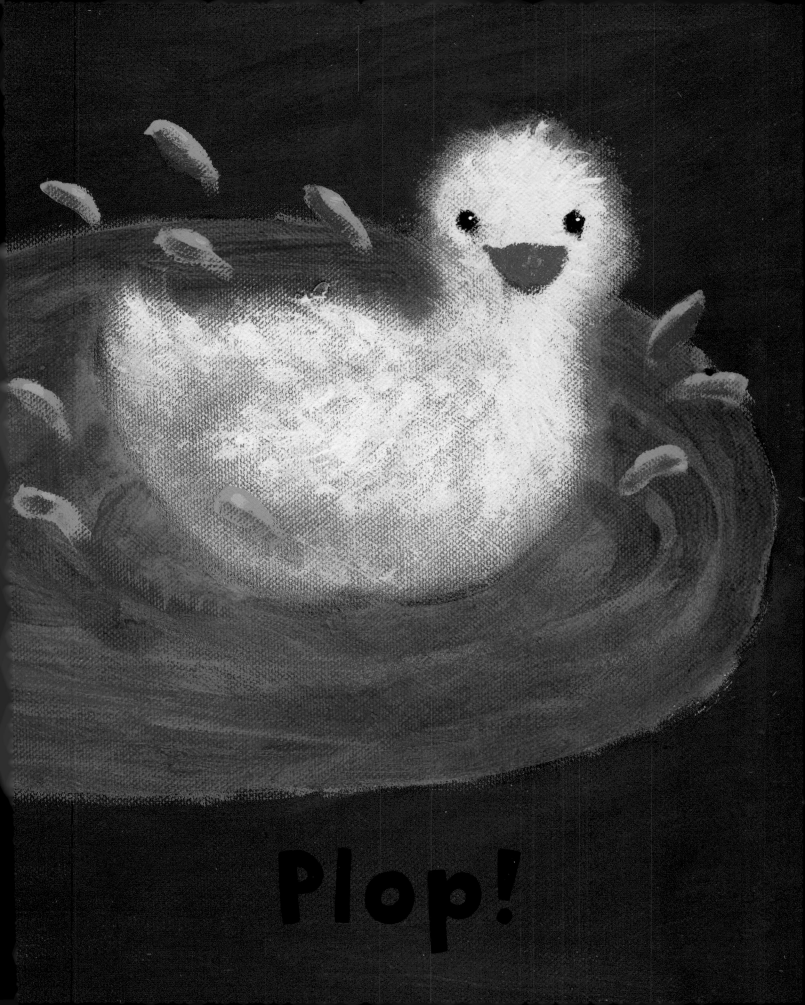

Plop!

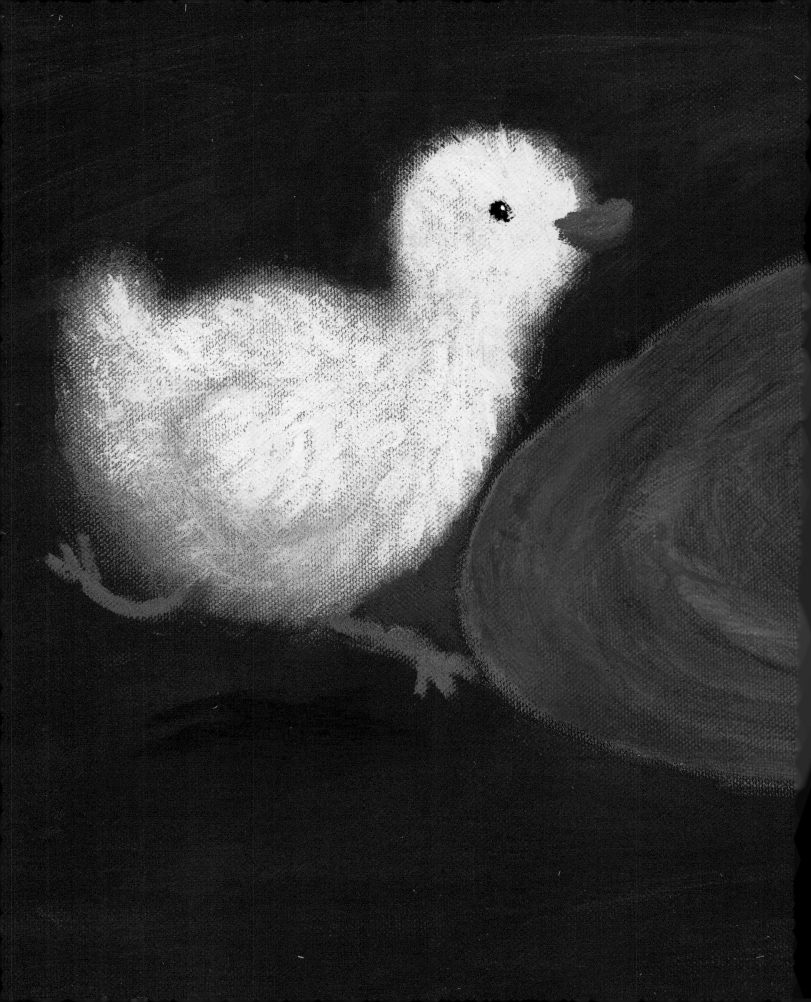

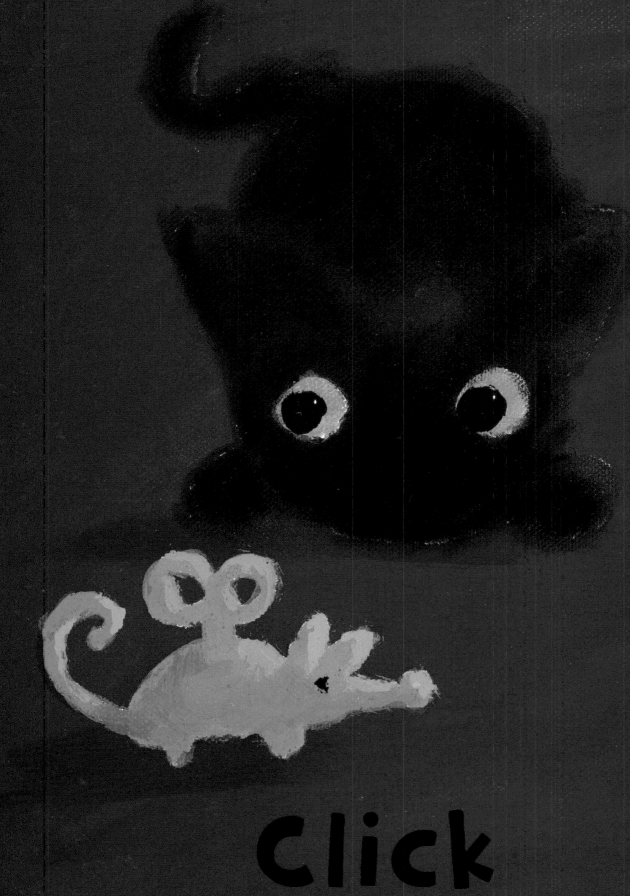

Click

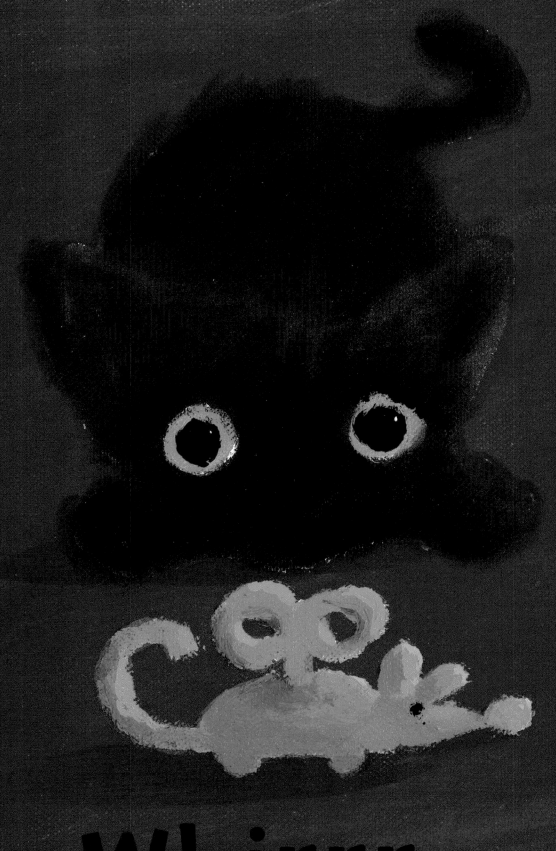

Whirrr...

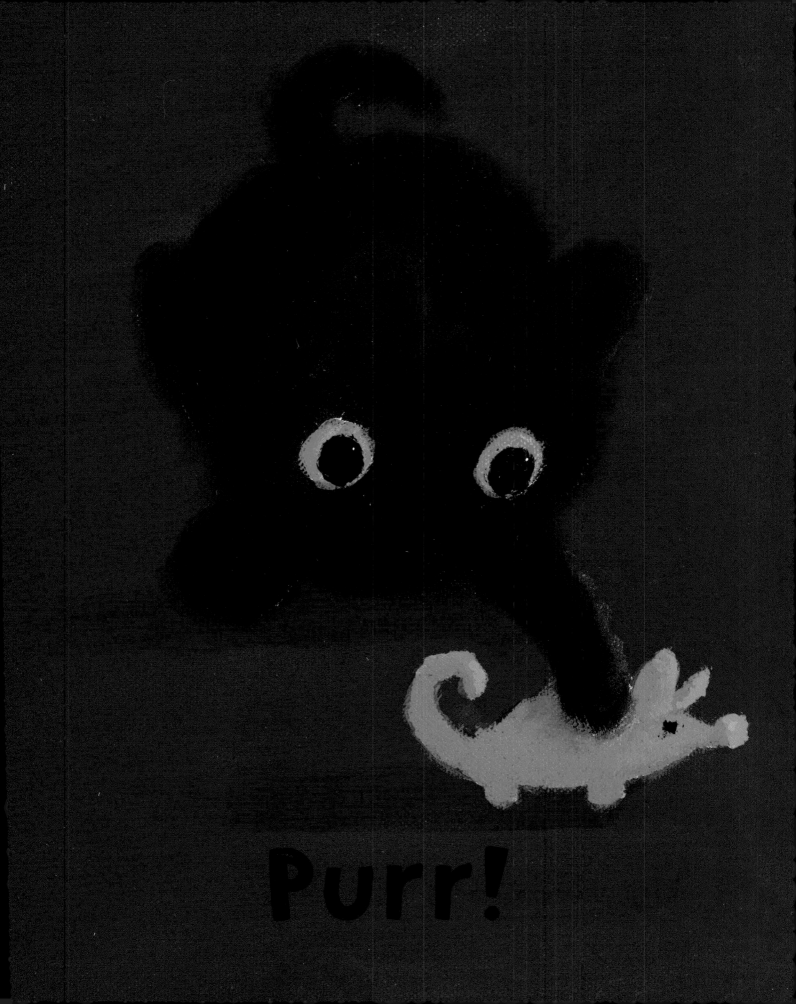

Purr!

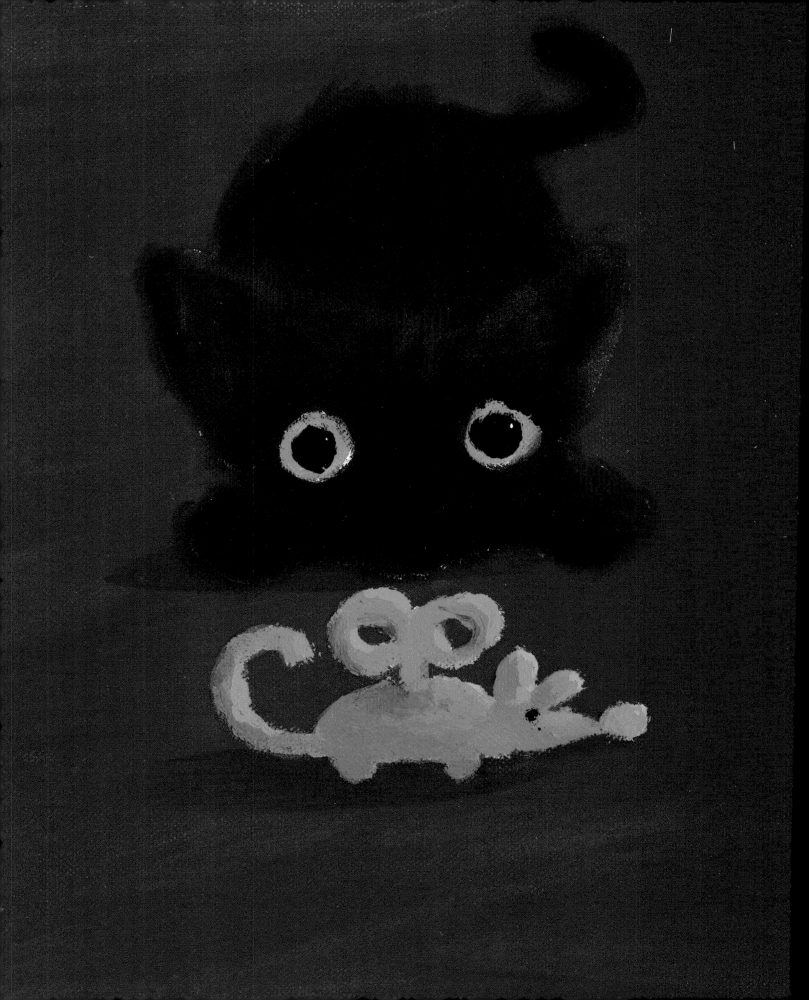

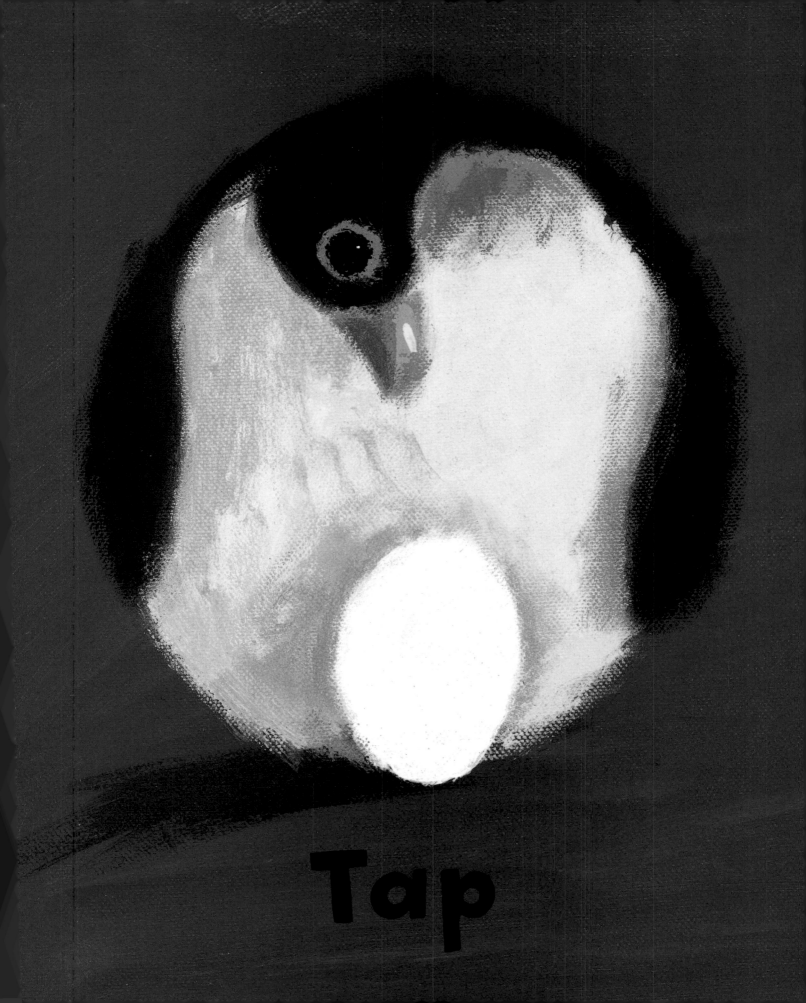

Tap

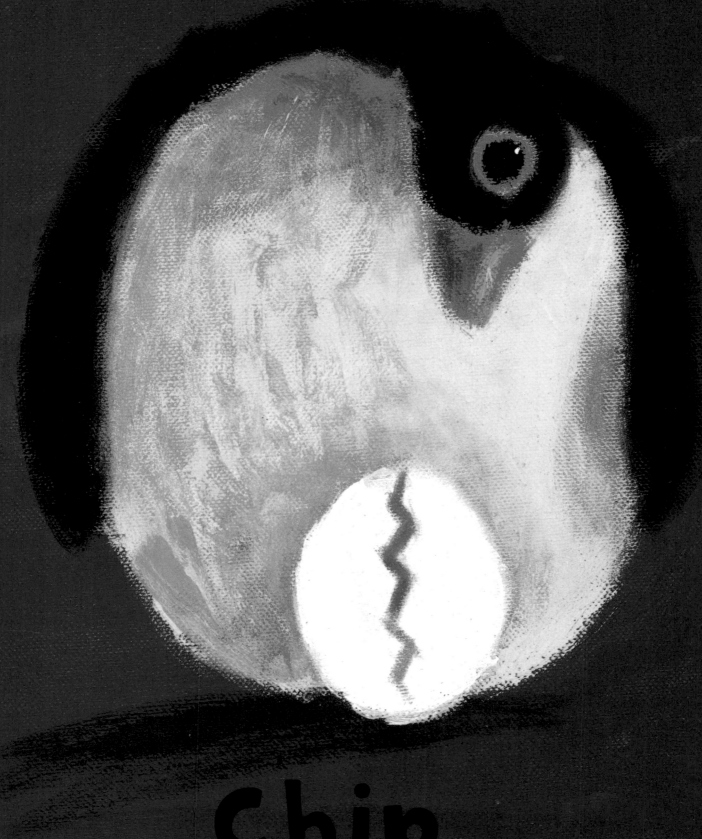

Chip...

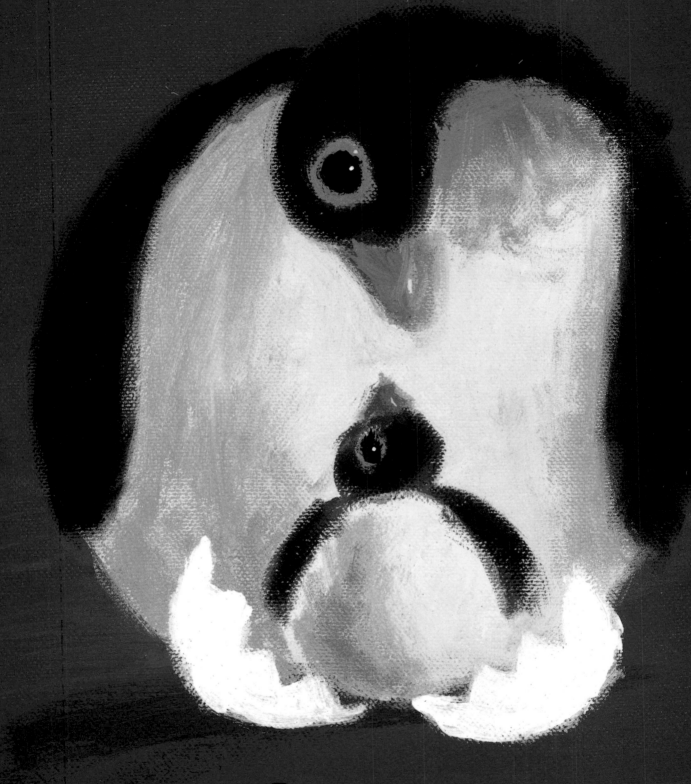

Cheep!

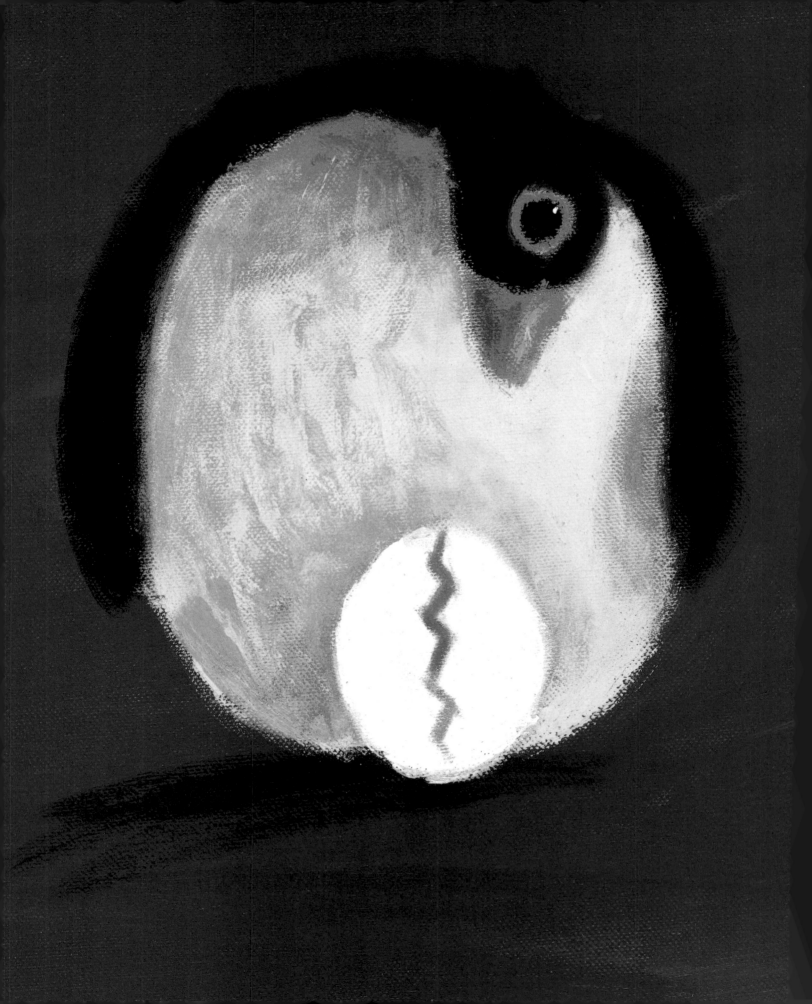

Sip

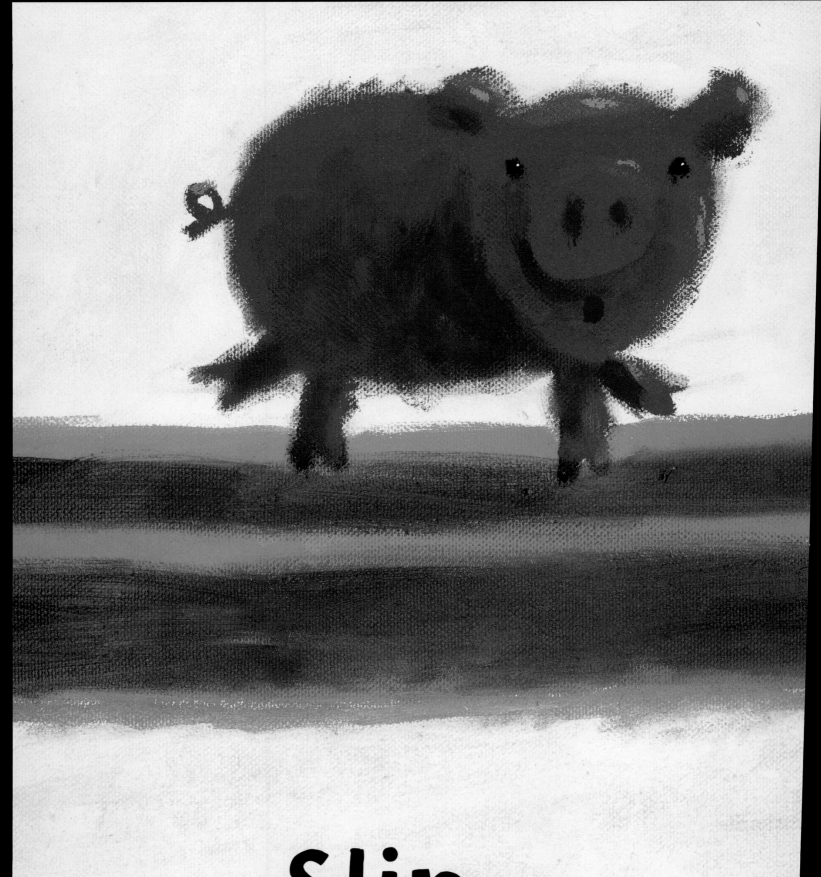

Slip...

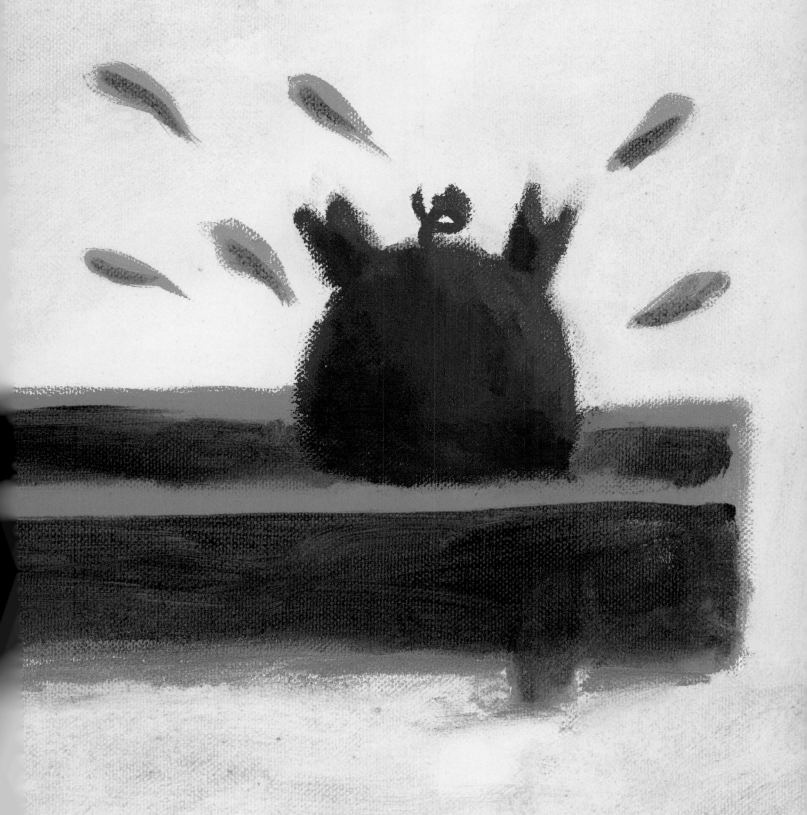

Squelch!

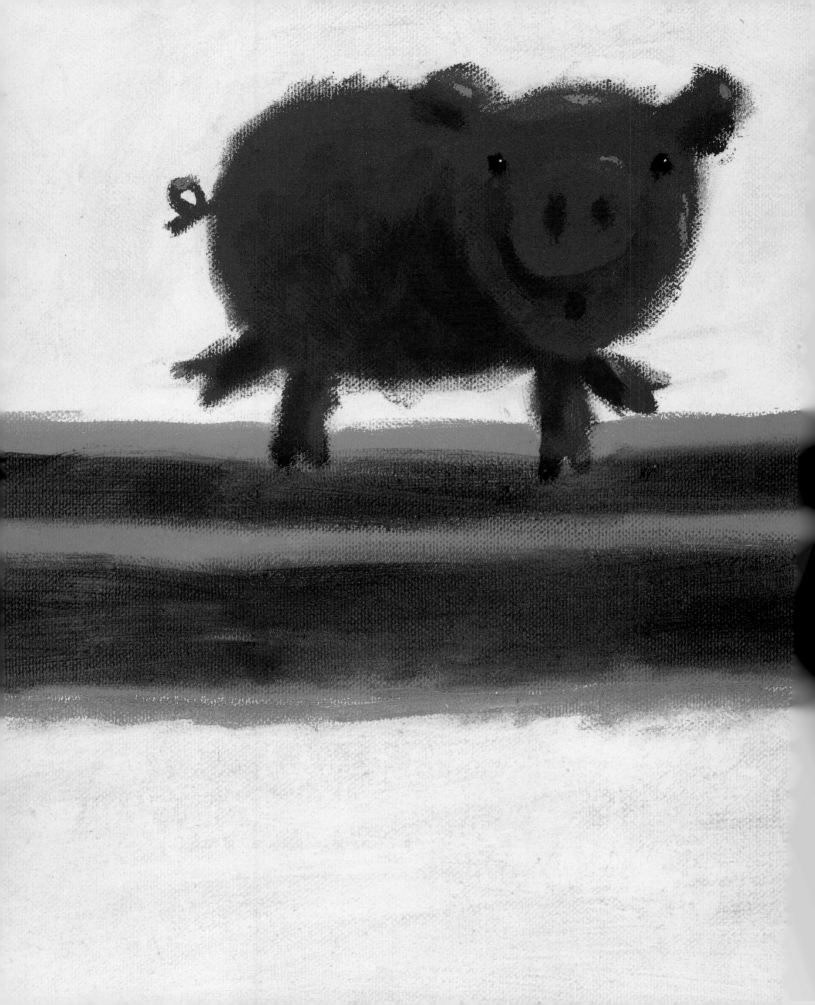

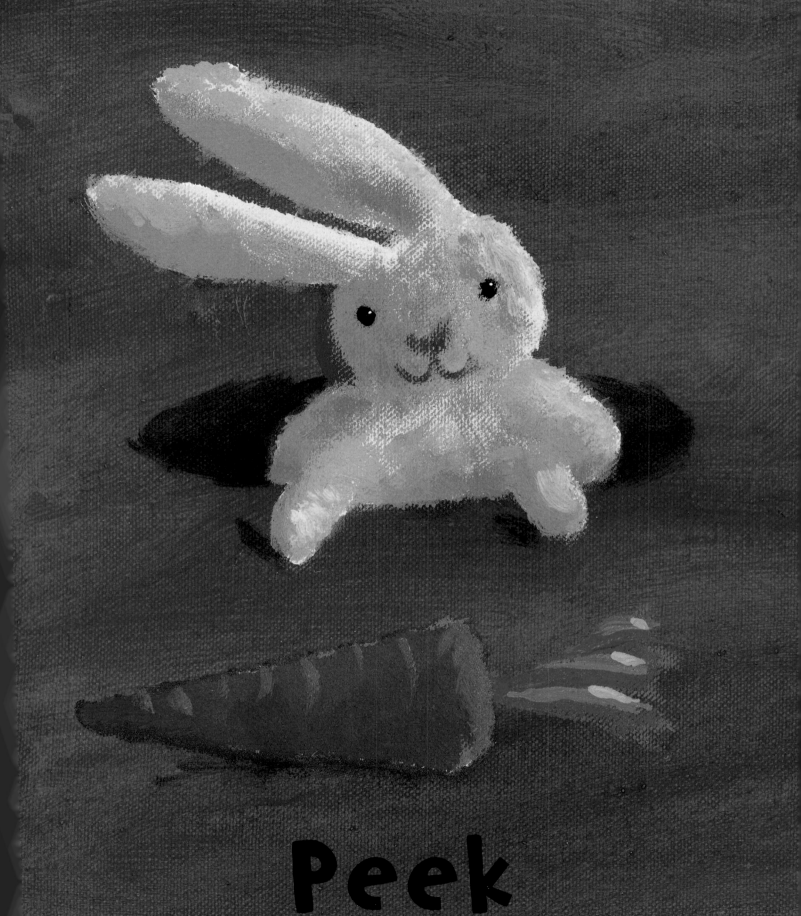

Peek

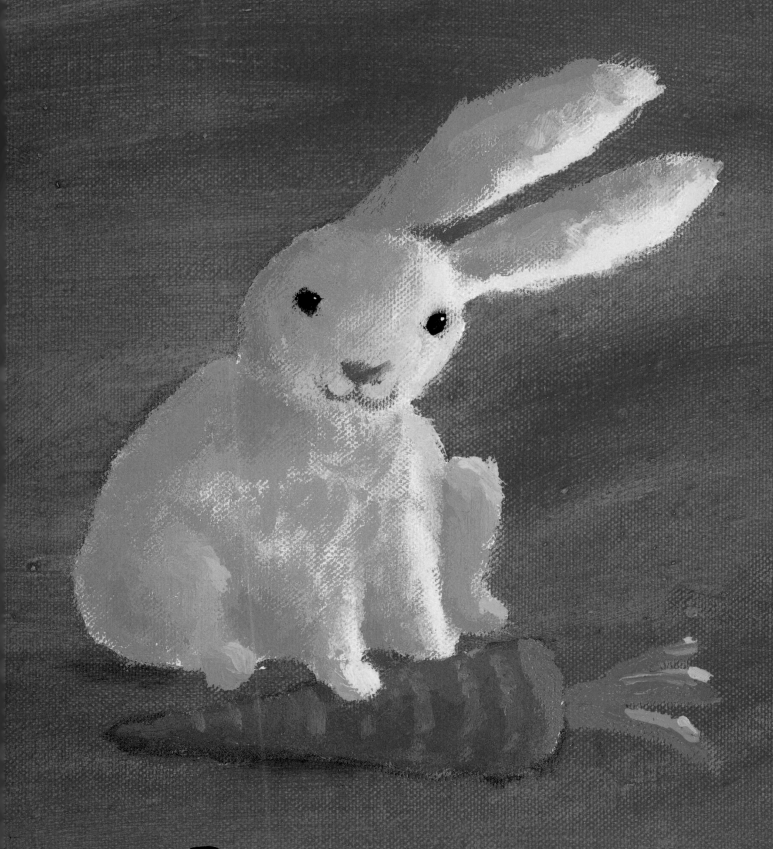

Pounce...

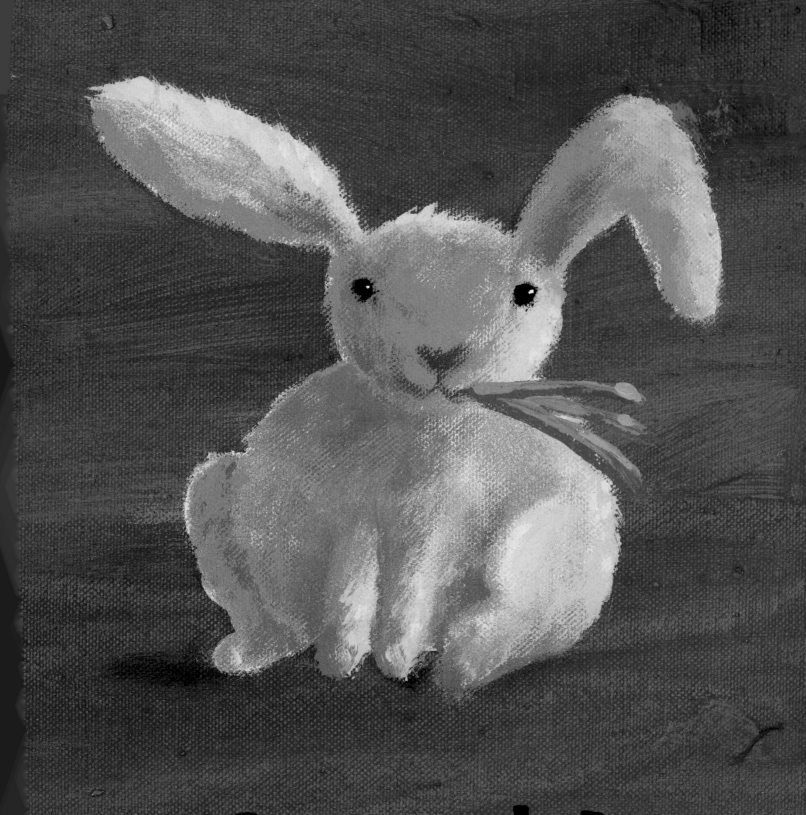

Crunch!

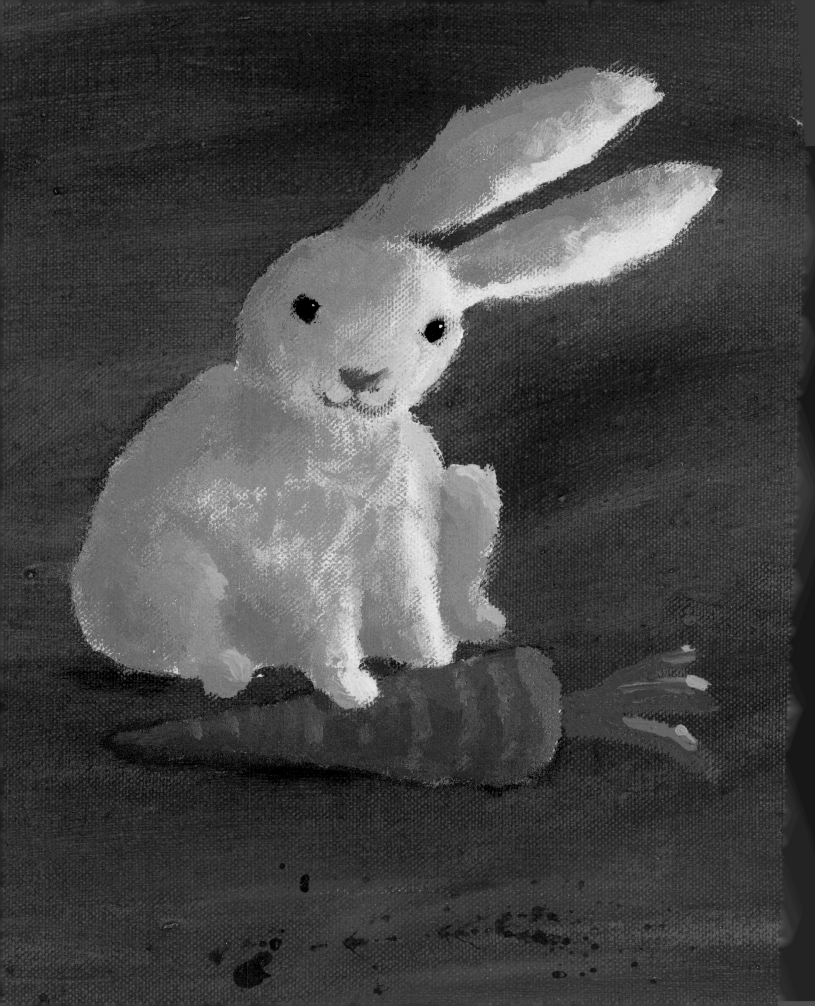

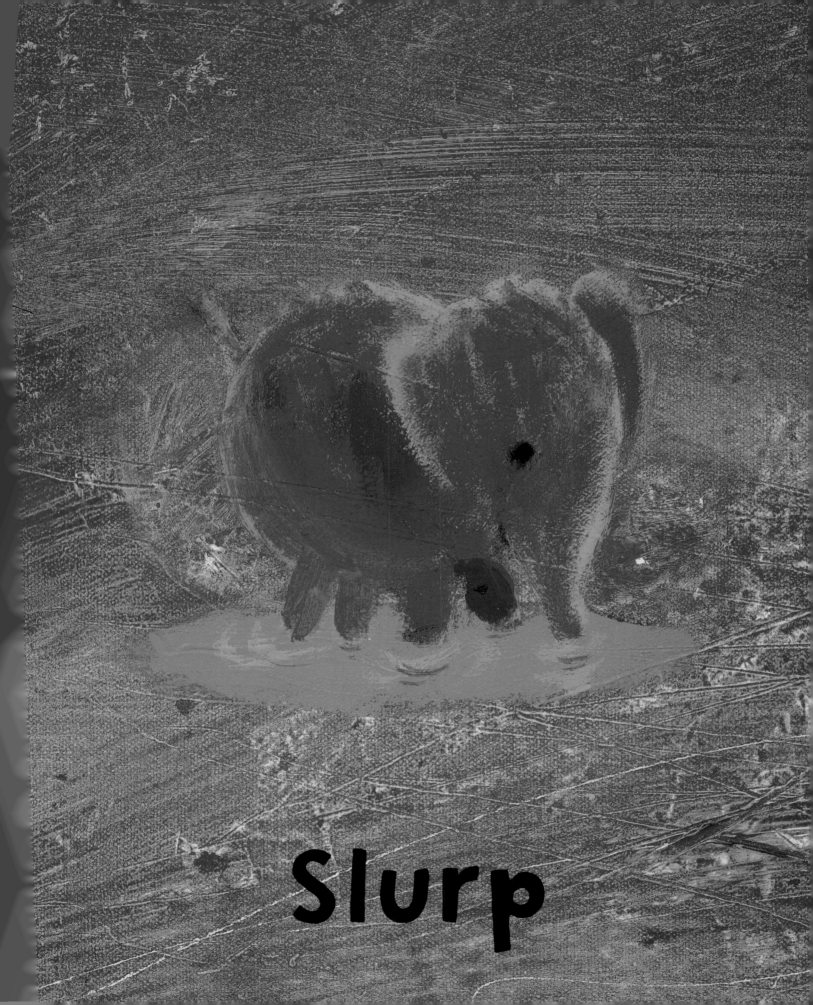

Slurp

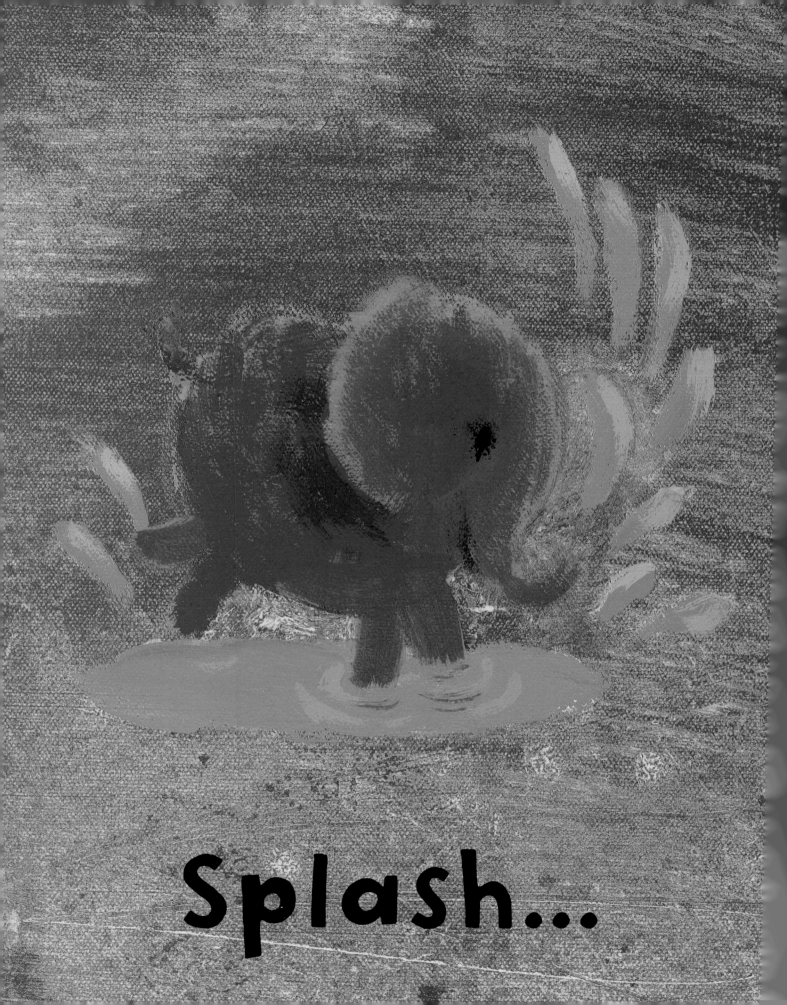

Splash...

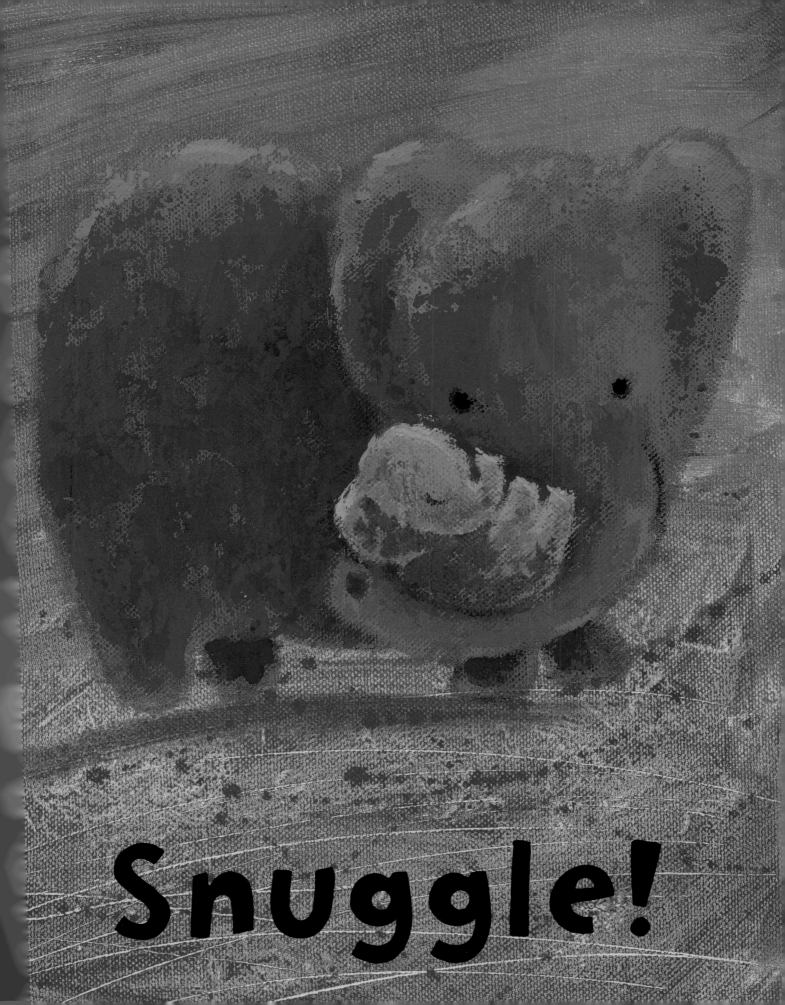

Snuggle!

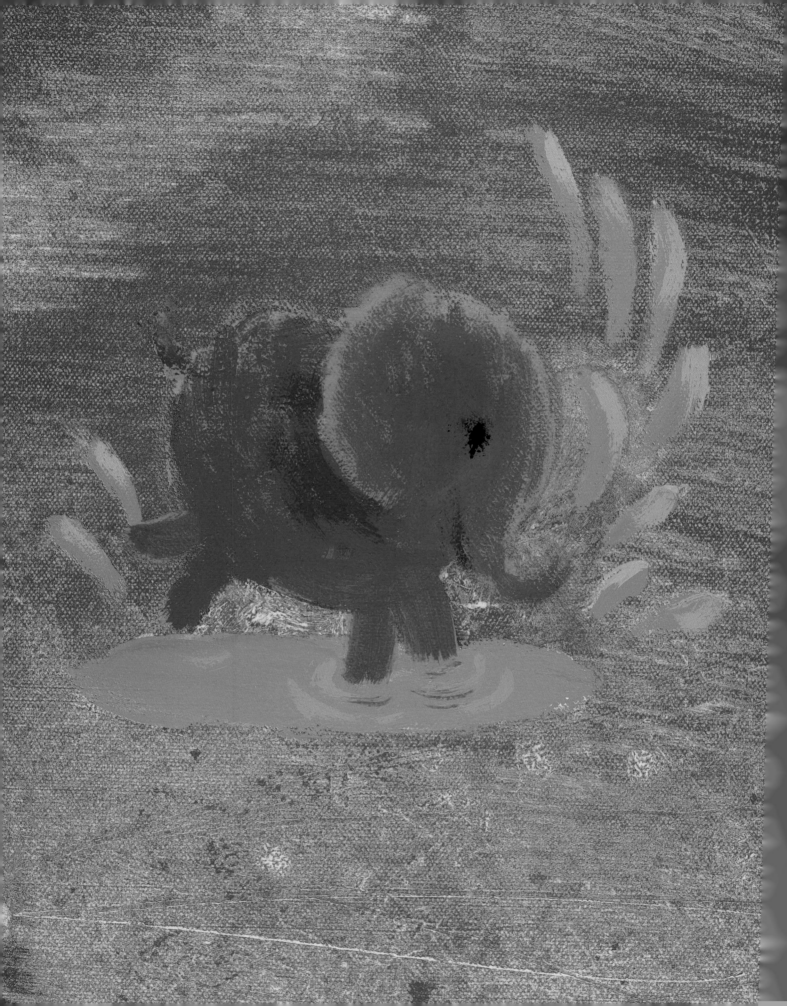

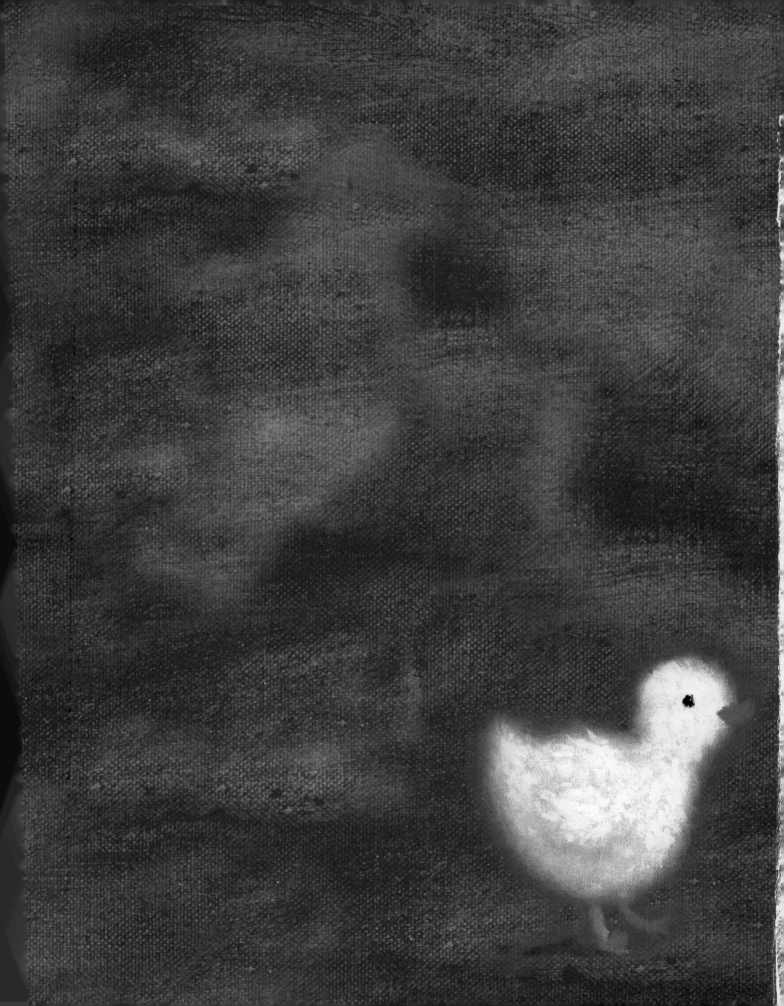